# Tuesday...
## A Lucky Day for Lars

by Joanne A. Reisberg     Illustrated by Nancy Cote

Tuesday...A Lucky Day for Luis

Written by Joanne A. Reisberg
Illustrated by Nancy Cote

Published by
Operation Outreach-USA Press
Holliston, MA

ISBN 978-0-9792144-8-6

Printed in the United States of America

MIX
Paper from
responsible source
FSC® C10352

For those Freeburg Boys
John, Jim and Charlie

And Special Thanks to my wonderful editor and publisher,
Judith Golden

J.R.


For Franky, Maggie, Casey, Mayday, Snowie and the
numerous loving pets that have been such a big part
of our lives.

N.C.

Luis spotted a dark car that had trailed his school bus for blocks. The yellow bumper sticker clued him in that he'd seen this same car last week.

As he stepped off the bus, the car slowed and parked by the curb. Those people didn't know the kind of third-grader they were dealing with. He was an alert kid. He knew all about adults asking for directions when they already knew the answer.

Luis ignored a twinge of fear. He was safe in his own neighborhood, wasn't he?

*Stay alert. Pay attention. Notice everything.*

He made a mental note… *dark green car, narrow crack in rear window, and that yellow school sticker on the left bumper.* If people inside acted scary, he could give this information to the police.

2

The car's front door scraped open. Luis's grip tightened on the strap of his backpack. He took a sprinter's stance, ready to run for help if anyone rushed toward him.

But that's not what happened at all.

The people inside the car tossed out a small brown rug. When the rug landed on four feet, Luis stared. "It's a dog!" he whispered. Sure. They let him out to go to the bathroom.

A hand inside the car waved at the dog. The small furry dog answered by wagging its tail. "Cute," Luis thought.

Then the driver spun his wheels…and sped off.

"Hey," Luis yelled. "Stop, you forgot your dog!"

Playfully, the dog bounded after the car. His big ears flopped up and down as he ran.

This didn't make sense. A sickening feeling swirled in the pit of Luis's stomach. It's not a bathroom break. The owner planned to abandon his dog.

Luis started running. "Come back," he shouted to the dog. "The people in the green car don't want you anymore."

Those cruel words slipped out before Luis could yank them back. With new-found energy, he pumped his legs and ran as if he were still in yesterday's field-day race.

After jogging for two blocks, Luis did the only thing he could think of. He stopped, puckered up his mouth, and blew a shrill whistle as Dad had taught him.

"Come back!" he hollered again. He dug in his backpack and held up a cookie. "I've got food for you."

The dog finally slowed. He stood for a while, head down, panting hard. With a turn of his head, he glanced one last time at the green car as it sped around the corner.

Luis waited for him to make the difficult decision. After a few seconds, it happened. Luis cringed when the dog looked his way. The droopy look on his face showed he understood exactly what had happened.

9

This dog knew in his heart that his owner didn't plan to come back.

The dog took his time trotting toward the sugar cookie.

Those ears didn't flop up and down. His tail didn't wag.

Brown fur, matted in a tight circle around his neck, indicated

he had worn a wide collar.

There was no collar, with a name on it, to hug his neck now.

Grrrrrr

"It's okay, little buddy. *You* know who you are. That's what's important. You're a smart dog. You knew when to stop running. I'm really proud of you."

Luis dropped on one knee and stretched out his hand. A low growl grew in the dog's throat.

"Hey, I'm your friend." Luis longed to stroke his fur. To rub his shoulders. To tell him he's not alone in this world. Instead, he put the cookie on the sidewalk and sat down on someone's front steps.

Luis thought about that car and his own bus stop. No one else ever got on or off at that corner.

"Your owner must have seen me last week. I think those people in the green car *chose* me to be your new friend."

Whether he convinced the dog or not, Luis searched his mind for a proper name for him. This guy wasn't the Buddy, Pal, or Rex type. He remembered his teacher reading about Robinson Crusoe, and naming a guy Friday. Only today was Tuesday. "Tuesday?" Luis said grinning at him.

The dog's floppy ears perked up.

"Hey, your real name might have started with a T. 'Tuesday' can be your name." Luis groaned. How would he feel if some kid said, "I'm changing your name?"

17

As Tuesday munched down the cookie crumbs, Luis noticed he had no scratches on his nose or face. His nails looked clipped. Tuesday's fur even smelled doggy clean. "You are one lucky pup. Somebody took good care of you. Sure, you'll miss your owner but you'll always have those memories in your head."

Luis's fingers reached out to brush Tuesday's fur. "You know, we're a lot alike. You miss your owner and I miss my dad. He's in the Army keeping us safe. But he's a long ways away. I'm proud of Dad but I still miss him. I'll email him tonight and tell him all about you."

Tuesday inched a little closer.

"My dad and I play Frisbee together. If you and I practice, maybe we can get good enough to enter one of those contests."

Luis rolled his eyes. How totally dorky he sounded, telling all this to a dog who couldn't answer back. But that's why dogs were so special. They listened no matter what a kid said. At least no one heard him blabbering on.

Luis glanced around to make sure. It was then he spotted Alex Hoffman behind him. *He'd been sitting on Alex's steps.* Alex, the smartest kid in his class who knew everything!

"Hey, Luis," Alex said heading toward him. "I didn't know you had a dog."

Tuesday's quick glance said, *"Don't tell him my owner doesn't want me."*

"I…I kind of found him. Thought I'd call him 'Tuesday'."

20

"Grrrrrr," Tuesday growled as Alex squatted down and stretched out his hand.

"His growl," Luis said, "is one of his best features."

Right then an awesome thought popped into his brain, the perfect solution to keeping Tuesday. If Dad kept them safe doing his job in Afghanistan, Tuesday could keep them safe here at home. Dad's deployment would last another six months. He should have thought of it sooner. Tuesday was definitely *guard-dog* material, and *good luck* had landed them both on Alex Hoffman's front steps.

Luis scooted over to let Alex sit down. "I don't know if my mom will let me keep Tuesday. I sure could use your help."

"Me?" Alex asked, gently patting Tuesday's shoulder. No growl escaped this time.

"See," Luis said. "He likes you already."

Alex reached for Tuesday's paw. "My mom had a dog named Skippy. We still have his blue leash hanging in our garage. This one's a Cocker Spaniel."

"Yeah, I thought so."

"They're bred to retrieve birds. Tuesday looks well cared for. Got a nicc silky coat, too. So your mom won't let you have a dog, huh?"

24

"Not unless…"

"Unless what?" Alex asked.

"Unless I can find a really good reason to keep him."

The plan spinning in his head would only work if Alex helped. Yeah, like that pin on his old wagon that kept the handle on. "Do you know what a linch-pin is?" Then he remembered who sat next to him. Of course the brain of the whole third grade class would know.

"Sure. It's the long pin in a bolt to keep a wheel from falling off."

Luis nodded. "You're right. You're kind of the linch-pin in *my* plan." If Alex couldn't help, it'd fall apart.

Alex's face turned serious. "What do you want me to do?"

Luis lowered his voice. "It gets dark outside around 7:30. I need you to rattle our door knob. Tap on a few windows. Then run like the time Billy O'Shoe won the school relay race. Tuesday will start to growl and my mom will say, 'What a great guard dog you are.' Maybe even decide to let me keep him."

"That's really clever. All right," Alex nodded. "I'll do it if I can walk Tuesday once in a while."

woof

Luis didn't hesitate. "It's a deal." They sealed their agreement with a high-five and two knuckle taps. "I've got a brown belt that's too small for me. Think it'll make an okay collar if I shorten it?"

Alex grinned. "Sure, and I'll ask my mom if we can use Skippy's leash."

Luis let his fingers brush against Tuesday as they headed down the sidewalk. Today, he and Tuesday had both found friends. "Tuesday, this is the way to your new home."

Luis thought he heard the tiniest bark that said, "Okay."

"I wish I could tell you about tonight…what to do, when to bark. But I can't. You'll do just fine. Don't worry about it." Luis knew those words were really meant for him.

"Mom," Luis called out entering the house. "I've got a surprise."

Tuesday trotted after Luis as he headed toward her desk. "I found a dog and named him Tuesday."

She glanced at Tuesday and then back to the computer screen. "He can stay two days."

"Tomorrow and the next day?" Luis asked.

"No. Today and tomorrow."

"Mom," Luis groaned, "what will happen to him then? He's got nobody. Nowhere to go. No place to stay." Choosing his words carefully, he told her about the green car at his bus stop and how unhappy Tuesday looked when it sped off. He couldn't use words about feeling "safer," or she'd suspect something.

"Today and tomorrow, Luis."

Luis didn't feel guilty about his plan. The reason was a good one: finding a place for a homeless dog.

"We'll need to buy dog food and fix up a place for him to sleep tonight," Mom said.

At seven o'clock, Luis sat on the bedroom floor with his arm around Tuesday. Together, they began watching the clock.

7:10. Luis drank a glass of water and hoped Alex would come on time.

7:15. Luis wiped his sweaty hands twice on a bathroom towel. "Mom? Think I'll do some homework." He needed the house as quiet as possible so Tuesday could hear the window rattle.

35

"Luis, are you feeling all right?"

"Sure. Fine. Maybe I'll just read to Tuesday. Spend special time with him."
His mom felt his forehead anyway. "See, I'm okay."

Luis realized he was too nervous to read. Together, they watched the
clock's minute hand.

It ticked 7:30...31...32...33.

*Grrrrrr*

By 7:44 Tuesday's ears perked up. Luis's heart began to race. Alex must have crept up to the house. *It's going to work.*

Tuesday's growl started low. It rumbled and grew and grew until huge barks echoed throughout the house.

Glass shattered on the tile floor in the kitchen.

Luis frowned. *Nooooo. That's not supposed to happen.*

"Luis, stay in your room!" In seconds, his mom grabbed her cell phone.

"Mom, wait!" Before he could stop her, she had called 911.

Tuesday raced toward the window, climbing over tiny shards of glass.

Luis couldn't believe he'd caused this to happen. It was his fault. All his fault.

Far off in the distance, the wail of a siren sounded. Now he'd never get to keep Tuesday

In twenty-five minutes, it was all over. Everyone had left but the police and a few neighbors. Luis stood with his mom and Officer Murphy on their front lawn. "You're lucky you have a guard dog, Ms. Fuentes. This is the third attempt we've had at a break-in in this area."

Luis knew he had to tell the truth. Tell that he asked his friend to rattle the windows. And he had to do it soon.

"Officer, this is my son, Luis."

"Well, Luis, your dog really helped us out this time."

40

Luis took an extra breath, ready to confess. *Say it…say it now*. Then he spotted Alex Hoffman running down the sidewalk and hurried over to him.

"Sorry, Luis. Mom wouldn't let me out of the house until I reviewed our challenge words for the spelling test. She expects me to be a grand champion like she was years ago and…"

"You mean you didn't tap on our windows?"

Alex shook his head. "So what's all the excitement? What's a police car doing in your driveway?"

Luis stood straighter than usual. He beamed with pride. "Our guard dog saved us all."

After the police left, Luis watched his mom carefully bandage Tuesday's paw. There was still time to email his dad. And tomorrow was soon enough to tell mom about what he and Alex had actually planned to do.

But everything had changed. Tonight's threat was real. Would his mom see that Tuesday, the best homeless dog in the entire world, had saved their family?

"Today and tomorrow," his mom had said about keeping Tuesday.

Maybe it could change to today, tomorrow…and forever?

## About Operation Outreach-USA

Operation Outreach-USA (OO-USA) provides free literacy and character education programs to elementary schools across the country.

Because reading is the gateway to success, leveling the learning field for at-risk children is critical. By giving books to children to own, confidence is built and motivated readers are created. OO-USA selects books with messages that teach compassion, respect, and determination. OO-USA involves the school and the home with tools for teachers and parents to nurture and guide children as they learn and grow.

More than one million children in schools in all fifty states have participated in the program thanks to the support of a broad alliance of corporate, foundation, and individual sponsors.

To learn more about Operation Outreach-USA and how to help, visit www.oousa.org, call 1-800-243-7929, or email info@oousa.org.